Daisy Pig

by

M. J. Robson

As told on *Jackanory*

Illustrated by Gillian Hulse

BBC BOOKS

For all my grandchildren
Freya, Anya, Luke, Poppy,
Rachel, Jade, Bronwen and Oliver

Published by BBC Books,
a division of BBC Enterprises Limited,
Woodlands, 80 Wood Lane, London W12 0TT
First published 1992
© M. J. Robson 1992
ISBN 0 563 36302 9
Illustrations by Gillian Hulse
Set in 12/15pt Century Old Style Roman
Typeset in Great Britain by Goodfellow & Egan, Cambridge.
Printed and bound in Great Britain by Clays Ltd, St Ives PLC
Cover printed by Clays Ltd, St Ives PLC

Contents

1   Daisy Pig Keeps Shop   7
2   Daisy Pig at the Seaside   22
3   Daisy Pig Goes to London   39
4   Daisy Pig – Nurse   54
5   Daisy Pig Goes Riding   74

Daisy Pig
Keeps
Shop

One day, as Daisy Pig walked through the village in her new hat, a notice in the sweet-shop caught her eye. It read –

WANTED. A reliable person to take charge of the shop this morning. £1.50 per hour to suitable applicant. APPLY WITHIN.

"Well, that's certainly me," said Daisy Pig, in her usual confident manner. "Whatever reliable means I'm sure I'm it," and without further ado into the shop she went.

"Good morning, Daisy Pig," said Mr Wood pleasantly. "Can I help you?"

"Not really," answered Daisy Pig. "You see – *I've* come to help you," and she pointed to the notice. "You require a reliable person. Well – I am *most* reliable. What's more, one pound, fifty an hour seems very suitable to me."

Now Mr Wood had had no response to his advertisement, and looking at Daisy he had to admit that she was a very smart pig, especially in her new hat.

"Well?" asked Daisy Pig, as Mr Wood hesitated.

"Are you sure you can handle money?" he asked a little doubtfully. "And give people the right change?"

"Of course I can handle money," retorted Daisy crisply, "and give people the right change. Now, if that's all, I'll start right away."

And so, rather to his surprise, Mr Wood found he had a new assistant. Daisy Pig removed her hat very carefully and tied the strings of an apron behind her in a very large bow.

"Everything's priced," said Mr Wood, pointing vaguely at all the shelves and jars and boxes, "and most people know what they want – but you can always advise."

"Certainly," agreed Daisy impatiently, wishing he would go away so that she could start being in charge.

"If you're sure you can manage –" began Mr Wood, still hesitant, but Daisy had already taken up her place behind the counter.

Mr Wood knew when he was beaten. "Very well," he said, turning to go. "I do have rather a lot of paper work to do. Remember, if you need help, I'm only next door."

But Daisy Pig was not listening. Already she was looking about her. Behind her, jar after shiny jar of sweets lined the shelves. To her right, boxes filled with chocolates or candies were arranged so that customers could see their pretty pictures, while, in front of her, lay all the delectable things that children love, such as liquorice boot-laces, toffee bars, lollipops, sherbet dabs, aniseed balls and gob-stoppers.

"Oh, what a lovely job!" she smiled happily. "To think I'm actually going to be paid for it! I should earn – let me think, there are still three hours till dinner-time so that should be – four pounds, fifty pence. Nearly *five* pounds, just for selling sweets!"

She smoothed her apron and without thinking popped a mint cream into her mouth where it melted like a dream. It was delicious!

So delicious, in fact, that she was about to help herself to another when the shop bell rang and in came two small girls.

"Yes?" inquired Daisy Pig, in her very best shop assistant's voice. "What can I get you? Aniseed balls? Lollipops?"

"No, thank you," answered one of the little girls politely. "We'd just like a chocolate cream egg each, please," and she pointed to a boxful beneath the glass counter.

"Oh," said Daisy Pig, "I hadn't noticed *those*." She handed one to each of the girls, took their money and made sure she gave them the correct change, but as soon as they had left the shop, she picked up one of the eggs and examined it. Even through the silver paper, such a rich smell of chocolate emanated that her little eyes gleamed, and her mouth watered.

"I wonder what they taste like?" she thought. "After all, what if people ask my advice? I really ought to know." At this point the wrapper seemed to fall off of its own accord and, within seconds, the egg was in her mouth, and chocolate was dribbling down her chin. Daisy Pig held her head to one side, thoughtfully.

"Mmm!" she sighed. "Blissful! But I *do* need to be absolutely sure . . .," whereupon she slipped another egg into her mouth, and then another, so that by the time she felt absolutely confident that she could recommend them to her customers, five chocolate eggs had disappeared.

The shop bell went again. Hastily, Daisy Pig licked her lips and then smiled, a rather gruesome, sticky brown smile, at the old lady who came in.

Fortunately, the old lady's eyesight was not too good. "Good morning," she said. "I wonder if you have any cough candy left? If you have, I'll have a quarter. Oh yes, I can see them," and she nodded at a jar behind Daisy's head.

"Certainly," Daisy Pig fluted graciously, and lifted

the jar down. As the lid came off, a very different smell assailed her nostrils. This time, it was a dark, warm, sugary, spicy smell. With great care, she weighed out a quarter of a pound's worth, slid them into a paper bag and handed them to her customer.

"I do like these," confessed the old lady. "Indeed, I'm quite a little pi- pi-, Oh dear," and she blushed. "What I mean is, I'm quite a glutton where cough candy is concerned. Are you?"

"I've never tasted cough candy," answered Daisy Pig, wondering, as she took the money, what a pi- pi- was.

"Then you simply must try them, my dear," smiled the old lady.

"Well – the customer is always right," Daisy told herself as the old lady left and she picked out a piece of candy and sucked it, rather cautiously at first. But she need not have worried for a gorgeous, hot, aniseed flavour filled her mouth and flowed down her nostrils until she positively glowed.

"How lovely!" she gasped and, putting in her hand, carefully extracted two more pieces before returning the jar to the shelf.

"What a simply wonderful job!" she told herself again as she sucked away industriously. And after that, every time someone came in to buy something, Daisy Pig felt it her duty to sample whatever was bought. She tried liquorice allsorts, and then sherbet dabs (only they made her sneeze!), and butterscotch and chocolate éclairs and sugared almonds. In fact, she tried almost everything but somehow or other she just could not bring herself to try the pink sugar mice with their long string tails.

She even explored one of the boxes of chocolates, first carefully slipping off its Cellophane wrapper and then sampling some of its contents; but only one person came in to buy such an expensive present and that was a man looking for a present for his wife.

"They really do look lovely," he said, gazing at the boxes. "I suppose you don't know what they're like inside?"

"But, of course!" answered Daisy Pig in a superior way. She picked up the box that she had opened. "I can certainly recommend these," she assured him with great confidence, "especially the orange creams."

"Can you really?" The man was most impressed and looked into the box that Daisy Pig had now opened before him. "But where are they all?"

"All what?" asked Daisy Pig, innocently.

"All the chocolates," retorted the man, a little crossly. "I can see only lots of empty spaces."

In some surprise, Daisy Pig looked into the box. She, too, could only see lots of empty spaces, mostly where once delicious orange creams had reposed.

"Looks as if someone's been eating them," said the man, and he seemed to be looking accusingly at Daisy.

Daisy Pig pretended to think hard. "Well," she said at last, "it most certainly wasn't mice," and she beamed sweetly at him.

But the man was not amused. "Mice! You've got mice in the shop?"

Daisy Pig nodded, "Oh, about a dozen," she said lightly. "But they really are lovely little things. All pink – with long tails."

The man exploded. "Well that's it!" he said, "I'm not having any chocolates from this place." And he hurried, indignantly, out of the shop.

"Fancy being afraid of little sugar mice!" said Daisy Pig, and eyed the half-empty chocolate box. She then sang happy little songs to herself and, in between finishing off the remaining chocolates, she dusted the shining jars with a little feather duster until the bell rang again and into the shop came a young boy for chocolate eggs.

Daisy Pig had forgotten clean about them. She bent down under the counter to see with dismay that there were only three of the lovely chocolate eggs left.

"Ah," she said, popping up again. "How about trying something else – like liquorice boot-laces?"

The boy's face darkened, and he scowled dreadfully. "I 'ate liquorice boot-laces," he said.

"Or lovely bulls-eyes?" she rushed on.

The boy turned a baleful eye on her. "I 'ate bulls-eyes," he said. "I want a chok-let egg. That is,"

16

he added with heavy sarcasm, "if *you* don't mind."

Daisy Pig was almost about to retort that she did mind when she remembered something about the customer always being right. With a snort of indignation she bent down, picked out an egg and placed it on the counter.

The boy eyed it for some moments and then he looked hard at Daisy Pig.

"'Oo said anything about one egg?" he demanded nastily. "Gimme two."

"Two?" Daisy Pig's heart missed a beat.

"Yeah – two," sneered the boy.

Gritting her teeth, Daisy Pig bent down and brought up a second egg which she laid beside the other.

The boy now surveyed the two eggs. For one dreadful moment, Daisy Pig thought he was going to ask for the third, but instead, he put his hand into his pocket, brought out a fistful of pennies, and counted the exact money on to the counter. Gathering up his eggs, he turned to leave. As he opened the door, however, he called back cheekily over his shoulder –

"Just you wait! I'll be back this afternoon for the other one, you'll see. I'm just going to get more money and I'll be back."

"Do you mean for this one?" cooed Daisy Pig, holding up the third egg.

"Yeah, that's it," smirked the boy. "So sucks to you – *Fatty*," he added most rudely.

"Oh, *what* a pity!" trilled Daisy. "Fatty's just bought it." And peeling off the silver paper, she popped it whole into her mouth.

With a howl of rage, the boy stamped out of the shop and disappeared down the street.

The very next person to arrive on the scene was Mr Wood himself.

"Why, Daisy!" he cried, looking about him. "You have had a busy morning!" His eye caught the empty chocolate egg box.

"Goodness!" he exclaimed in delight. "I thought I'd never get rid of all those eggs. You must have had some very good customers this morning." He looked at Daisy whose face, he thought, had a peculiar stripy look about it. "Are you all right, Daisy?" he asked kindly.

"Perfectly," replied Daisy Pig, a little faintly. It occurred to her that she could easily tell Mr Wood who his very best customer had been!

"Good!" smiled Mr Wood, feeling very cheerful indeed. "Well, here's the four pounds, fifty I owe you. Thank you for being such a splendid help. If you'd just check the till first, you can lock up and then go home."

As he toddled back upstairs whistling happily, Daisy Pig was looking gloomily into the till. It was four pounds short exactly. With a sigh, she took the four pound coins out of her wages and put them into the till. She then locked up and set off home. Her chin was striped with chocolate trails, a dab of sherbet rested on the end of her nose, and a piece of toffee had glued itself to her ear.

As she walked, she reflected, a little sadly, that she had only fifty pence in her pocket to show for her morning's work. But – and a smile spread across her face as she licked the last trace of chocolate from around her mouth –

– it was almost lunch-time!

Daisy Pig

at the

Seaside

10 Minute
Sun Tan
Lotion

One day, Daisy Pig was watching Sally, Farmer Jones' daughter. Sally had come into the garden and chosen the very spot where the sun blazed down the most.

"I'm just going to sunbathe, Daisy Pig," she said. "Do you like my bikini?"

Daisy Pig looked at Sally. There seemed very little of the bikini and a lot of Sally.

"I want to get a good tan," explained Sally. "Then when I go to the beach I shan't look as white as a peeled onion. Everyone there is so beautifully brown."

"What's the beach?" asked Daisy Pig, very interested.

Sally looked surprised. "Haven't you ever been to the seaside, Daisy? Everyone goes there in the summer. You lie on the sand to get as brown as you can and swim in the sea when you're hot. It's very fashionable to be a beautiful brown."

When Daisy Pig went home she looked at herself in the mirror. She was very, very white. "How dreadful!" she thought. "I'm not fashionable at all. Perhaps I should buy myself a bikini and go to the seaside too."

She looked in her little piggy bank. Besides the fifty pence she had earned in the sweet-shop, there were several pound coins that her Great Aunt Matilda Pig had given her for her birthday.

"That should do," said Daisy hopefully and putting the money in her purse she trotted down to the shop.

The young assistant brought out several bathing suits for her to try on, but none looked like Sally's.

"I want one," she said, "that's in two bits, if you have such a thing."

"Oh! You mean a bikini," the assistant said. She looked a little surprised, but brought out one in red, one in blue and then one in green with a pattern of white dots all over it.

"I'll have *that* one," said Daisy Pig in her usual decided way.

"It's certainly very smart," agreed the young assistant as Daisy Pig held it against herself and looked in the long mirror, "and once you've got a tan you'll look most elegant in it."

"Of course, I intend going to the seaside," said Daisy Pig, who could not help showing off as she viewed herself this way and that in the mirror.

"Then there's no problem," smiled the assistant. "A week by the sea and you'll soon be very brown."

Daisy stopped preening herself. "I hope it won't take that long," she said. "I can only spend one day on the beach."

"Ah, well, you must get some good sun-tan lotion from the chemist," advised the girl helpfully. "Oh – and some sun-glasses to protect your eyes."

Now Daisy Pig had heard of neither of these things before, but smiling very sweetly she said, "I'm so glad you reminded me, I had quite forgotten!"

As soon as the bikini was wrapped up and paid for, Daisy Pig hurried off to the chemist.

She purchased a bottle of Ten Minute Sun-tan and then tried on the sun-glasses the chemist offered her. Instantly the world went dark.

"Who's put the sun out?" cried Daisy, in some alarm.

"It's only the effect of the glasses, madam," said the chemist soothingly, as she removed them from her nose. "They're to protect your eyes from the glare of the sun. Now is that all?"

Daisy, feeling rather foolish, admitted that it was, but as soon as she had left the shop clutching

her various parcels her spirits rose and she began to prance down the street, full of the joy of the adventure that lay before her.

"Wot's up with that Daisy Pig?" muttered Milly the cow looking up from her feed. "She got ants in her pants or something?"

The geese came running after her making a fearful racket, wanting to know what she was carrying, but Daisy ignored them all until she met Vic, the cart-horse, who had his head hanging over the gate.

"I shan't be able to visit you tomorrow, Victor," called Daisy importantly. "I shall be catching – " she waited for the geese to draw nearer – "I shall be catching the ten o'clock train to the seaside."

Vic was most impressed. He had heard of the seaside before, but no one he knew had been there.

"What are you going to do there, Daisy Pig?" he asked in great wonder.

Daisy Pig looked around at all their blank faces and smiled.

"Goodness me!" she exclaimed in pretend surprise. "Don't you know? Why, I shall lie all day on the beach in my bikini –" Here she held up the tiniest parcel for their inspection – "until I'm the most *beautiful* brown!"

Vic was too mystified to speak but the geese, thinking of their own white plumage, cackled in disapproval. "What ever *do* you want to go brown for?" they demanded.

Daisy Pig froze their noise with a glance. "Because it's *fashionable*, that's what!" and off she bounced,

nose in air while her neat little feet stotted off the road like hailstones.

"Fashionable?" snorted Milly the cow, who had been sidling nearer and nearer until she was now close behind Vic. "If she wants to be brown why don't she jus' roll in the muck like 'er ol' dad used ter do? That's wot I wanter know." She sniffed hard and the geese cackled with laughter.

But Vic remained loyal.

"If Daisy Pig wants to go to the beach an' get brown all over, an' be fashionable," he said firmly, "then 'oo's goin' to stop 'er? That's all oi wanter know," with which he turned back to the never-ending business of keeping Farmer Jones' grass cropped.

The next morning at ten o'clock the villagers, all of whom seemed to have windows in need of washing or steps in need of sweeping, were stunned by the appearance of Daisy Pig teetering down the street in a pair of high-heeled red sandals. She was wearing a very floppy straw hat, loose white jacket, and an enormous pair of dark sun-glasses. One hand was carrying a large beach bag while the other rose in a cheery wave to all her friends. And each time she waved, the white jacket fell open, revealing two of the tiniest strips of green and white spotted material – and a great deal of Daisy Pig. Vic the cart-horse groaned inwardly and closed his eyes but the gasps of shock and horror about him fell like music on the ears of Daisy Pig.

"That'll give 'em something to talk about," she chortled and throwing them a last radiant smile she wobbled jauntily into the station. The train was almost ready to leave, but the guard, seeing such a smart, fashionable lady approach, showed Daisy Pig into an empty carriage.

"Thank you, my good man," she said graciously, as he touched his cap to her, and settled herself comfortably in the corner. Just as the train pulled out of the station she caught sight of innumerable faces hanging like wilting flowers over the railings. Immediately, Daisy stood up and blew kisses. The faces fell back in confusion. With a grin, she sat down again, opened up her bag, took out a cheese and onion sandwich and bit into it.

The seaside was a most thrilling sight! There was the sand she had heard so much about – soft golden and warm – and there was the sea, making lazy little sallies towards the children who were busy building castles and forts on the firm, wet shore.

Daisy Pig chose a nice, clean spot for her deck-chair and after removing her white jacket and red shoes sat down. She could not help noticing the heads that turned in her direction and the many admiring glances that came her way.

Even the sun sparkling on the waves took a little time off to throw warm little kisses at her.

Daisy Pig was incredibly happy. As she lolled lazily in the chair, from behind her large, dark sun-glasses she surveyed the crowds. Mothers and fathers sat with their shrieking children and ate jam sandwiches

liberally coated with sand. Young girls, in clusters of
twos or threes, lay in their bikinis, a few as white as
Daisy Pig but most the colour of ripe hazelnuts. The
oil on their skin glistened. Oh! Daisy Pig remembered
her bottle of Ten Minute Sun-tan. Opening her bag
she carefully removed the bottle and applied the
lotion to every reachable bare part of her anatomy.
The young men around her rolled closer. She
flounced up the frills on the tiny skirt of her bikini, lay
back, and gently closed her eyes.

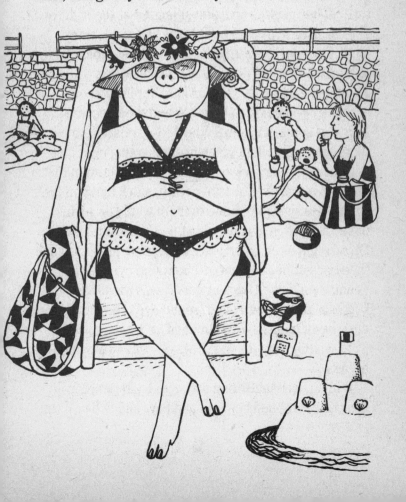

Daisy Pig was blissfully happy. Time passed, the sun rose higher in the sky and still Daisy slept. Sometimes, a little snore bubbled from between her lips almost waking her but never quite. She began to dream. She dreamed she was sitting by her fireside on a winter's night. As she dreamed it seemed the fire was growing redder and redder and hotter and hotter until . . . In a sudden panic she sat up. Wide awake. To her relief she found herself still on the beach. But the burning sensation still continued. She tore off her glasses and almost fainted at the sight of herself. Her body was bright pink! Bright lobster pink! Everywhere the bikini was not – was pink, and although she could not see her own face she could see a pink haze that rose from around her little snout.

She looked quickly about her and then became aware of something else! The people nearest to her were strangely silent and while the young men were still gazing at her, it was not with the admiration that greeted her arrival. A faint bacony smell hung on the air and every so often one of them would lift up his nose and sniff in a manner that was most unpleasant. Daisy Pig looked down on her steaming pink form and then back at her audience. The round eyes of the young men looked back at her. It was then that she began to think their round, round eyes reminded her of something else – of fried eggs, of fried eggs on a plate waiting only for the slices of – one man wiped his lips.

With an ear-shattering screech, Daisy leapt from her chair, grabbed her coat and bag, and fled into the

sea. The water sizzled as it came into contact with her hot body but on she went, plodging as fast as her little legs could take her, away from the horrid crowd that had followed her to the very water's edge. On and on she went, only daring to come out onto the shore when she reckoned it safe to do so.

Now her bikini skirt hung in sodden folds, and trails of green dye ran down her legs. Throwing on her white coat, she walked barefooted and bare-headed (for both shoes and hat still lay beneath her deck-chair) down to the station. The guard, not recognising in Daisy the vision of loveliness that had greeted him only that morning, shoved her into an already over-crowded compartment. But, fortunately, the sea had cooled her down. Nobody's nose wrinkled in that dreadful manner of the people on the beach. No one looked at her with fried-egg eyes. Indeed, no one looked at her. They only trod heavily on her bare toes, and squashed her so tightly that at times her eyes almost crossed.

But Daisy was past caring. If only, she was thinking desperately, I can get home without anyone seeing me! Life, she knew, would not be worth living if Millie the cow so much as glimpsed her! Fortunately, dusk was falling as the train pulled into the station, and once out she forsook the High Street along which she had earlier flaunted herself, slipping quietly along the darkening back lanes until she reached her own dear little house, where she opened the door with great stealth. Suddenly, torch-light shone upon her. She jumped in fright.

"Hello, Daisy!" came a deep, familiar voice and then followed a gasp as the light fell full on Daisy's face. "What *'ave* you been doin'?"

It was Vic. Daisy buried her face hastily in the collar of her coat.

"Why are you so red?" persisted Vic innocently. "Oi thought you'd gone to the seaside to get brown?"

"I'm not well," said Daisy in muffled tones. "I've – I've got a fever. That's it – I've got a fever. Don't come any nearer," she cried in a panic as Vic moved. "And *will* you put that *torch* out!" she added sharply.

Vic lowered the torch. As he did so, the light fell on Daisy's green mottled legs and then on her bare feet. Vic was slow but not stupid. "Very well – oi'll see you tomorrow then, Daisy," he said. "Oi just wanted to see you safely home like."

Daisy viewed him through a button hole. "Thank you, Victor," she said gratefully. "Do come tomorrow. But Victor – I'm really too ill to see anyone else. You will tell them, won't you?"

"'Course oi will," said Vic faithfully. "Oi'll see no one disturbs you. You 'ave a nice bath, Daisy, and mebbe you'll feel a lot better by tomorrow."

The door closed. Vic turned away and made his own way home. Tomorrow, he thought, he would hear the whole story. And then the vision of Daisy's dirty bare feet and green and red legs came into his mind and he began to titter and then to chortle and then to laugh and then to roar.

"Oh, Daisy Pig!" he cried, as he broke into a quick trot, tears running down his hoary old cheeks, "Oi *do* love you."

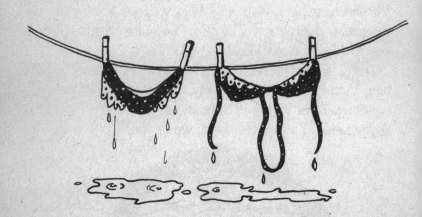

Daisy Pig

Goes to London

Daisy Pig,

One day the postman brought Daisy Pig a letter from an old friend, Feral Fox. Feral used to live in the village of Wilmanstone but had for several years now, lived in London since when Daisy and her Great Aunt Matilda had heard little from him. It was rumoured, however, by many in the village, that he was "doing very nicely" and was "quite the gentleman these days", and so Daisy Pig opened the letter with great excitement.

Dear Daisy, it read,

Sorry not to have written to you more frequently, but life here in London is quite hectic! Still working at night but making enough to enjoy myself through the day. And so I wondered if you'd care to spend the day with me in the big city? Lots of things to show you. Do come! What about next Tuesday? Drop me a line if you're coming, and the time of your train, and I'll meet you at Victoria Station.

Yours affectionately, Feral.

Daisy could scarcely contain herself. A day in London! It was almost too wonderful to be true! Quickly, she wrote a letter of acceptance to Feral and sped off to post it.

On the way back she met Vic and with great

excitement poured out her news.

"You're not going there to get brown, are you, Daisy Pig?" he asked cautiously.

Daisy was quite cross at being reminded of her last trip to the seaside.

"Certainly not!" she retorted and added stiffly, "One goes to London to *see* things."

"Wot things?" asked Vic curiously.

Daisy had no idea.

"*Lots* of things," she said, frostily, and turned to go.

"Well, oi only asked," said Vic placidly, "cos next Tuesday, the others are sure to want to know what you're doing up in London. 'Specially Milly the cow!"

Daisy stopped. She had intended – quite casually of course – to let everyone in the village know about her trip. But now she saw how much more interesting it would be to keep them all guessing.

She drew her plump little body up to its full height. "In that case," she answered, slowly fluttering her eyelashes in a way she felt suggested mystery, "they'll just have to wait. *Won't* they?" with which parting remark she glided away.

The following Tuesday was a lovely fine day. Daisy put on a white dress of pure silk, a straw hat trimmed with rosebuds, white shoes, white gloves, and carried a large pink handbag. One glance in the mirror told her that she had never looked lovelier. With great glee, she set off for the train. This time, the street was empty except for one young goose who, seeing Daisy, stuck his head through the fence and chanted, "Look who's coming down the street, Daisy

Pig on her plates of meat!"

Daisy Pig, who prided herself on her neat little trotters, appeared not to have heard a word and he was just opening his beak to repeat his rude little jingle when her large pink bag caught him smartly on the head, causing him to bite his tongue. "Ough!" he squawked, and quickly withdrew his head but, by the time his tongue had ceased smarting and his eyes watering, Daisy was almost out of sight.

The train to London was much faster than the one that had taken her to the seaside, and field after field, and village after village, flew by before giving way to rows and rows of little houses, and then bigger and bigger buildings until finally the train came to stop in the most enormous station! Daisy got out and wobbled down the platform. There was so much noise! And so many people! More than she had ever seen in her life! As she handed in her ticket to the collector, she wondered what she would do if Feral Fox was not there to meet her. But to her great relief an old familiar voice called out: "Daisy! Daisy Pig!" and there was a tall ruddy-faced gentleman, coming towards her.

"You look gorgeous!" he said, and gave her a peck on the cheek. Daisy Pig looked at Feral and her spirits rose. He was so elegant! He wore a grey jacket, silk shirt, cream waistcoat and striped trousers, and was carrying a silver topped cane. "Something to eat first?" he suggested. "Before we see the sights of London?" and Daisy, realising that she had not eaten since breakfast, agreed heartily.

They walked out into the hustle and bustle of the city. Feral, holding Daisy's elbow in a most gallant fashion, led her down the street, across the road, and into an elegant hotel where their footsteps were lost in the thick, soft carpets. They entered the restaurant where a waiter showed them to a table and left a menu card with them.

As they sat down a large gilt framed portrait hanging on the wall caught Daisy's eye.

"Oh, that's the Queen," Feral informed her casually. "You know – lives in Buckingham Palace."

Daisy was dazzled. She looked at the Queen, resplendent in her diamond tiara and with large diamond earrings.

"Good place for grub, you know," drawled Feral. "The Palace, I mean. I often call in there for an evening." He picked up the menu card and was just about to hand it to Daisy when his eye caught the words – *Grilled Pork Chops*.

"Excuse me," he smiled at Daisy, "but would you allow me to choose for you?"

"Of course," said Daisy, thinking how charming he was. She leaned back comfortably. The smell of

delicious food was tantalising and her mouth kept
dribbling so freely that she had to keep dabbing it with
a woefully inadequate hanky. Worse, little chomping
snorts would keep bubbling up in her nostrils.

Feral scanned the menu. *Roast goose*. *His* mouth
began to water now. *Honey-baked hams*. He looked
up at Daisy who smiled back innocently.

The waiter reappeared and Feral said, rather
loudly, "I don't think there is anything here the lady
would like but I do think you might have something
special in the kitchen?" He lifted an eyebrow and
stared meaningfully into the waiter's eyes.

The waiter looked at Daisy, looked back at Feral –
and said, "Ah – yes, sir. We do have a very special
dish that I'm sure the young lady would enjoy."

"Good," smiled Feral, showing his back teeth, "and
for me I think I'll have – " and his finger pointed to the
roast goose.

"Very good, sir," said the waiter, his left eye
dropping slightly, and off he went into the kitchen.

"Roast goose for the gentleman at Table 22," he
bawled above the clamour of pans and lids. "And a
bucket of swill for the lady!"

Minutes later, a huge bowl of what appeared to be
mixed vegetables, beautifully garnished with parsley,
was placed before Daisy, while a gorgeously roasted
bird, discreetly trimmed, was set before Feral.

Daisy's mouth was watering freely now. So was
Feral's. As they tied their napkins around their necks
their eyes met. Feral held up his glass of wine. Daisy
held up hers. And then their heads went down. Feral

44

worked with his knife and fork until he'd removed every scrap of flesh and then he picked up the bones and gnawed and growled, and growled and gnawed. Daisy, who had given up trying to stop the snorts and grunts of pleasure that trilled down her nose as she truffled her way through the delectable mess before her, was soon scraping the bottom of the dish. At last they both stopped. Feral leaned back and looked at Daisy. A piece of potato peeling was clinging just above her eye. Her snout was littered with fragments of bread, carrots, cabbage and custard. Daisy looked at Feral.

His large tongue was licking away the last remnants of orange sauce and goose fat. They both sighed, great sighs of utter contentment.

"How about some ice-cream?" suggested Feral.

"Lovely!" breathed Daisy ecstatically, and began to clean up her face with her napkin.

"With cherries and chocolate?"

"Delicious!" And Daisy sighed yet again.

A few minutes later she asked dreamily:

"What was the name of the dish I've just eaten?"

"Oh – *that*!" Feral had to think hard for his head kept telling him it was time for a nap.

"Oh yes! That was – that was *Chef's Special*! You were lucky. Very lucky! He has to be in a good mood to make that dish up. It – it's very complicated. Yes, indeed!"

"Goodness!" exclaimed Daisy, trying to smother a yawn. "I was fortunate!" and she settled down to her ice-cream.

"Coffee in the lounge, sir?" asked the attentive waiter. Feral nodded. Four hours later, they woke up. Two cups of cold coffee stood on the table in front of them. Feral looked at his watch and then shot to his feet.

"Quick, Daisy!" he cried. "We've just got half an hour to catch your train!"

"Wha – what's that?" enquired Daisy sleepily.

"Come on," urged Feral. "We'll be able to do it nicely if we go now."

"But what about all the things we were going to see?" protested Daisy.

"Another time, old girl," answered Feral, helping her to her feet. He straightened her hat, picked up her gloves, and hurried her out of the restaurant.

They just made the station in time.

"Awfully sorry you didn't see much," grinned Feral as Daisy climbed aboard the train. "But I did enjoy your company."

"Don't worry," smiled Daisy, "I've had a scrumptious time!"

"Come again, soon," called Feral, waving.

"Love to," cried Daisy, waving back furiously.

The train, gathering up speed, hurled itself into the country and Daisy snoozed gently in the corner seat.

At Wilmanstone station, Vic was there to meet her. "Had a good time?" he greeted her.

"Gorgeous!" smiled Daisy, thinking of the *Chef's Special*.

"See lots of things?" he went on, eagerly.

"What things?" frowned Daisy Pig.

"Well – oi dunno," said Vic, taken aback. "Only you've been up in London all day. Oi thought that's why you'd gone! Everyone's wantin' to hear about your trip an' all. Oi mean, ol' Milly the cow, her cousin went up to London an' he saw Hyde Park, an' Piccadilly Circus, an' the Changing of the Guard an' oi dunno what else."

For a moment Daisy panicked, but then a strange gleam came into her eye.

"Didn't you see none of those things, Daisy?" asked Vic plaintively.

"No," said Daisy cheerfully and stepped out jauntily. Vic followed heavily in her footsteps. He was worried.

"But wotever are you goin' to tell everyone tomorrow? No one'll believe you went to London!"

"Won't they?" asked Daisy Pig, pretending to be surprised. "That's a pity. Because I saw something better than all those things." She turned round so suddenly that Vic had to jump backwards to avoid a collision.

"Wotever was that, Daisy Pig?" he asked, hope beginning to arise in him.

"I," said Daisy in a very clear voice, "*I* saw the Queen!"

Vic's eyes popped.

"What's more," went on Daisy, her voice still rising, "she was in the very same restaurant that Feral and I were in –" Vic's jaw dropped. " – and she had the most lovely diamond thing on her head, and huge diamond rings in her ears, and she kept smiling at us the whole time!"

Vic was speechless.

"Tomorrow –" said Daisy Pig, with the light of battle in her eyes, "we'll see if Milly the cow's cousin can do better than that. Now hurry up, Victor," she went on bossily, "and we'll have a nice cup of tea."

As they were sitting quietly by the fire, having finished their tea, Daisy, who had been fiddling with her ears and occasionally touching her head, turned and said, "Victor, how d'you think you get to be Queen?"

Vic stood up. It was time, he knew, to be going home.

Daisy

Pig~

Nurse

One day, Sally was going to visit her grandfather who was in hospital with a bad leg and she asked Daisy Pig to accompany her. Daisy had never been into a hospital before and she felt quite excited at the prospect. They both took posies from the garden and the prettiest "Get Well" cards they could find in the village shop.

Sally's grandfather was in a large, sunny ward filled with flowers.

"Hello!" he greeted Sally. "I see you've brought me a visitor."

"This is Daisy Pig, Grandfather," said Sally and kissed him. They pulled two chairs up to the bedside and chatted. Sally's grandfather told them that he was very much better and beginning to enjoy himself. He pointed to the locker by his bed.

"Look what my visitors have brought me! Enough fruit and chocolates to open a shop! Oh, help yourselves, girls – there's far too much for me. In any case, I'll probably be going home in a day or two. Go on," he said, seeing them hesitate, "enjoy yourselves."

Sally and Daisy needed no further telling, and soon

were tucking into his grapes and chocolates, while Grandfather joked with the nurses who looked so smart in their uniforms. Daisy Pig noticed the way they shook the thermometers and wrote little notes on the clip-boards at the bottom of each patient's bed. Once a doctor came to the next bed, rocked on his toes, and said with a great beam, "And how are we today, hm?" Daisy was most impressed. She especially liked the "hm?" bit.

When she got home, she made herself a cup of tea and sat down by the fire thinking how jolly it would be to lie in bed and have tea brought to her. But how, she wondered, did one become a patient? She got up and looked at herself in the mirror. A very healthy Daisy Pig looked back. Suddenly a far better idea came into her head. Not for her to be a patient lying in bed all day. No – she would be a *nurse*!

It was such an exciting idea that she rushed out of the house and hurried down the road that led to the farm in order to tell Vic. But to her surprise he was not to be seen anywhere in the field. Milly the cow was at the far end looking up inquisitively, but Daisy had no intention of telling *her* a thing. Off she went into the farmyard and looked into the stable, but Vic was not there, only the farm cat, warm in the straw.

"Have you seen Victor anywhere?" demanded Daisy.

The cat blinked. "He's not here," he yawned.

"I can see that," snapped Daisy. "Do you know where he might be?"

"Try his house," was all the cat would say before

curling up into a very cosy ball and going back to sleep again.

Daisy was surprised. Victor at home! That would be unusual, but off she sped to Vic's little house which was made of planks of wood and had stable doors so that if he chose he could watch the world go by. But both doors were closed.

Daisy knocked.

No answer.

She knocked louder and listened. A voice came faintly from within.

"Who's there?" it quavered.

"It's me," called Daisy. "Daisy Pig. May I come in?"

She heard heavy footsteps come shuffling towards the door which opened, and there was Vic, looking awful!

"Victor!" cried Daisy Pig, stepping in and shutting the door behind her. "What ever is the matter?"

"Oi'm not well," groaned Vic, collapsing into his easy chair.

"Not well?" Daisy Pig could scarcely believe her luck. Instantly, she was alert. "Now you've not to worry, Victor," she said in a very firm voice.

Vic groaned inwardly.

"Oi'm not worrying," he mumbled.

"Just you rest there in your chair –"

"Oi was resting in the chair," he reminded her, "until you came bang, banging on the door."

But Daisy Pig ignored his protestations. "Just you rest there," she repeated, "until I get something I need."

Vic looked up unwillingly at Daisy. A fierce light was burning in her eye. She was glowing with boundless energy. She was, it seemed, growing bigger and bossier every moment. He felt even more unwell.

"Wot oi'd really like," he said plaintively, "is a nice cup of tea and something for my 'ead."

"Certainly not," snorted Daisy, her back stiffening.

"Oi'm not asking for the crown *joowells*," he said bravely, but Daisy held up a hand to silence him.

"I can't do anything yet," she told him. "It's got to be done properly," and with that she left, leaving Vic to listen as her footsteps beat out a sharp retreat on the path outside.

For a moment he thought of making a dash for the door and escaping to the safety of his field but the slightest movement made his poor head thud. With a groan of despair he sank deeper into his chair and waited.

After what seemed like an hour but was, in fact, no longer than ten minutes, Daisy Pig returned. As she came through the door, Vic prised open an eyelid. His jaw fell. Daisy Pig was standing before him dressed in a blue striped frock, a white starched apron and with a white starched cap on her head. In one hand she held a black bag, in the other a board to which were clipped sheets of paper. "Now," she boomed heartily, bearing down on the cringing Victor, "and how are we today, hm?"

Vic tried to rally his nerve.

"Oi dunno how *we* are," he said, testily, "but oi know how oi am. Terrible!"

"Good," beamed Daisy. "Now let's see what the trouble is."

She grasped Vic by the wrist and at the same time studied her watch carefully. She then wrote on the clip-board, "Twenty past three".

"Wot are you writing, Daisy Pig?" asked Vic fearfully.

"Notes for the doctor," answered Daisy Pig. "*Not* for the patient's eyes."

"Oh!" Vic turned a shade paler.

"Now let's see if we can find out what the trouble is," said Daisy Pig.

"Well – oi've got this splittin' head –" began Vic, but again Daisy Pig stopped him with an imperious gesture.

"*I'll* tell you what's wrong with you," she informed him sharply, "not you," and lunging forward, she grasped his ankles and pressed hard. "Does this hurt?" she asked. Vic said nothing. Daisy pressed his knees. Vic tittered. She pressed his chest and then his shoulders. Vic giggled. Rather crossly, Daisy rapped him smartly on the head.

"Ouch!" cried Vic, and tears started from his eyes.

"That's it!" cried a triumphant Daisy Pig. "You've got a headache, Victor."

"'Course oi've got an 'eadache," he said when finally his eyes had stopped smarting, and the hammering in his head had eased off. "And if oi hadn't had an 'eadache before, oi've certainly got one now!"

"So all you need," swept on Daisy, ignoring his whining, "is an aspirin –"

"Ooh, yes, *please*," cried Vic, " – and a nice cup of tea."

Within five minutes, Daisy and Vic were both sitting round the fire enjoying a cup of tea.

"D'you know wot?" said Vic, moving his head carefully. "Oi think my 'eadache's goin'."

Daisy sat up in alarm.

"Oh, Victor!" she exclaimed. "It mustn't go yet. You've got to have visitors first!"

"Visitors? What ever do oi want with visitors?" he demanded. Daisy put her cup down.

"Don't you know, Victor? They bring you things. Nice things – like chocolates and sweets and grapes. They make you feel better."

"But oi am feeling better," Vic objected. "My 'eadache's almost gone!"

"Oh, no, it hasn't," Daisy Pig told him and gave him a sharp tap on the head with her pencil.

"Ouch! Ooh!" Vic groaned, his eyes spinning like Catherine Wheels.

Daisy Pig surveyed him with satisfaction.

"Still sore?" she cooed.

"'Course it is," said Vic crossly. "You've made it come on again, ooh . . . ooh . . . ooh."

"Good!" Daisy rose, straightened out her apron and arranged her cap. "Now I'll just put a notice on your door –"

"Oi ain't got the plague," protested Vic. "At least oi

hadn't before you came."

"– to say you're too ill to see visitors –" went on Daisy Pig, quelling him with a steely eye, "but would appreciate get-well gifts." She quickly printed out the message, signed it "Nurse Daisy Pig" and, stepping outside, pinned it on Vic's front door. Next she put a rather large cardboard box by the step. "That should do the trick," she said, confidently, coming back and sitting down again. "All we've got to do now is wait. When your friends have been we'll have a feast."

She stoked up the fire, fixed the blanket round Vic, and soon they were both snoozing gently, stirring only occasionally as the sounds of shuffling, or squeaking, or grunting outside reached dimly into the little sitting-room.

About tea-time they both woke up.

"D'you think they've been?" asked Vic, who was feeling peckish.

Daisy Pig got up and went to the door. No one was about in the street but the box certainly had things in it. Daisy carried it in, a smile of satisfaction caressing her features. Vic grew excited.

"Ooh, do hurry up, Daisy Pig," he cried. "Let's see wot's in it." Daisy put the box by his chair and Vic put his hand in. Out came a large turnip, slightly mouldy at one end. A card was attached saying *Love from Milly the Cow!*

"Oh – that's nice," said Vic loyally, but his face fell.

"Let me see," said Daisy rather impatiently. She plunged in her hand. Up came a bone, half-chewed and still with earth clinging to it from where it had recently been dug up. It was from Johnny the dog.

"Lovely," said Daisy Pig coldly, shaking the soil off her hand, distastefully.

"Well – we could make soup," suggested Vic helpfully. Daisy froze him into silence and put her hand in again, this time a little more carefully. Up came a dead mouse, attached to a card with "Best Wishes" written on it from the stable cat. She dropped it quickly back into the box.

"It's no good," she snorted. "They've got entirely

the wrong idea about what gifts to bring patients. I would have thought they'd have known *that* much."

"P'raps you should've told them, then," said Vic. "P'raps," and a light gleamed in his eye, "p'raps you've gone and made a mistake, Daisy Pig."

The thought cheered him up no end.

Daisy turned on him but not in anger. "You're right, Victor!" she trilled. "You're absolutely right! I'll empty those things out and then we'll see!"

Before Vic could protest, the box was turned upside down on his clean larder floor and Daisy Pig was scribbling an addition to her note which now read, *Frute, Flours and Choklets most welcome*.

"I'm glad I thought of that," she said, with a flourish of her pencil. "Now let's see if it works," and out she

65

bounced, disposing both box and note by the door.

"How about another cup of tea while we wait?" she asked, closing the door behind her.

Vic, who had just been going to remind her that it was *his* idea, changed his mind. "Yes, please, Daisy Pig," he said eagerly.

Daisy Pig looked at him suspiciously.

"I hope you're not feeling better?" she demanded. In reply, Vic gave a little moan. He most certainly did not want another rap over the head from Daisy's pencil. He groaned again.

"No-no!" he said faintly. "It's just that oi would so much like a cup of tea. For my achin' 'ead, you see."

Daisy's expression softened and she nodded in sympathy. Soon they were both back in front of the fire, relaxing in the warmth and enjoying their tea.

And then Daisy paused. Someone was coming down the street, not one of the farm animals, someone with shoes on. The footsteps halted by the door. After a moment, Daisy could hear things being put in the box and then the footsteps started up again and moved off.

Vic sat up a little straighter. Daisy Pig shushed him. When the footsteps had died away altogether, she tiptoed to the door, opened it, looked up and down the empty street, and then brought the box in.

"It's quite – heavy!" she puffed, dropping it down by Vic.

"Ooh-hoo!" chortled Vic in anticipation, and in went his hand.

Out it came clutching a large box of chocolates.

"Oh Daisy," he cried excitedly, "look at this!" but Daisy already had two hands in and was bringing out oranges, and apples, and then a bag of toffees, and then a card.

"Here you are, Victor," she cried triumphantly, piling them up on the table beside him. "And there's a card too."

Vic's face was alight with pleasure. "Oi've got one too!" he grinned. "It was with the choklets."
He opened the card and began reading it slowly.
"With love from Sally. Hope your leg's better soon."

"Isn't that nice!" cried Daisy Pig enthusiastically, slipping the other card quietly into her pocket. "Yes, isn't it!" agreed Vic, but he was looking very puzzled. "Oi wonder why Sally said leg?" He began to look round for other cards.

"Aren't you going to eat your chocolates?" fussed Daisy. "After all, head sounds very much like leg, doesn't it? Sally probably just mis-heard."

"Oh *you* told her!" Vic looked very pleased. "Was it when you went out to get your nurse's uniform?"

Daisy smiled discreetly.

"Come on then," said Vic jovially. "Come and help me eat these chocolates!"

Daisy willingly joined him and soon they had eaten most of the chocolates, sampled half of the toffees, and eaten two apples and an orange a-piece.

Vic leaned back in his armchair and sighed contentedly.

"Oi never knew how nice it was to be a patient," he murmured sleepily, his eyes half closing.

Suddenly, they shot open.

"Oh," he cried, "oi'd almost forgotten! What does your card say, Daisy Pig?"

"What card?" said Daisy innocently.

"You know," said Vic, "the one you put in your pocket."

"Oh!" Slowly, Daisy took the card out of her pocket. She opened it very carefully – and then smiled. It read, *To the best-looking patient of them all, from all the nurses in Ward Ten.*

Vic could scarcely believe his ears. The best-looking patient of them all! From all the nurses?

"You told 'em, too, Daisy?" he asked, looking at his friend in admiration. "You told the nurses in the hospital all about me?"

Daisy coughed modestly, and said nothing.

"Fancy you telling 'em about me," said Vic, wagging his head as if he could still hardly believe it. "Well, oi think oi'll have that nap now," he said happily. "You just stay there, Daisy, and you help yourself to my things."

His eyes closed and silence settled on the room, silence that is, apart from the sounds of Daisy Pig steadily wading her way through the chocolates, the toffees, and the fruit.

Suddenly the noise stopped. The room was so still that Vic opened one eye. He looked at his nurse. She was looking decidedly odd, her face changing from green to white and back to green.

Daisy stood up and wobbled slightly. "Now you're awake, Victor, and feeling better –" she said, turning even greener, " – I think I must go home."

"Are you all right, Daisy?" asked Vic interestedly.

"All right? Of course I'm all right," she answered, and walked with slow dignity to the door.

But once there, she flung it open and without so much as a goodbye, raced out, one hand pressed to her mouth, the other just managing to bang the door behind her.

Vic listened to the click-clacking of her speeding feet until the sounds died away.

"Strange," he said, frowning, as he settled back in his chair. But then his eye caught sight of the debris beside Daisy's chair, toffee papers, an empty chocolate box, apple cores, orange peel . . . and he chuckled.

"Oh, Daisy Pig," he said to himself. "Oi think it's my turn to come and nurse *you*."

Victor put on his old woolly hat, wrapped his muffler around his neck and then, reaching up onto the shelf above the kitchen sink, brought down a large bottle filled with some white stuff. It had an equally large label which said *Whizz Bang Stomach Pain Remover*.

"That should do the trick," he grinned, and opening the door, set off into the night, in the direction of Daisy Pig's house.

Daisy Pig Goes Riding

One day, as Daisy Pig was returning home from shopping, her ears caught the lightest of sounds, a dancing of sounds, very much like that of raindrops on a window pane. Turning round, she perceived the cause, for coming ever nearer to her was the most wonderful creature she had ever seen. It was a young horse, dapple grey in colour, with a proudly arching neck, a tossing mane, and four black hooves that shone like patent leather.

Daisy gasped in admiration. Goggle-eyed she watched as it pranced and danced towards her, and then a voice, less than magical, but cheery and familiar, called down to her.

"Wotcher, Daisy Pig! And how d'you like this old nag then, eh?"

Startled, Daisy glanced up and there, perched on the back of this wondrous steed, was Jack, Sally's elder brother, grinning down at her for all the world like the Cheshire Cat in *Alice in Wonderland*.

"I'm just taking her down to the paddock," went on Jack. "Going to put her through her paces. If she's any good, young Sally can take her to the Gymkhana next Saturday. Why don't you come down to the paddock and watch? See you there," and with a nod,

he rode off.

For once in her life, Daisy had no ready answer. Her mind swam with all these unknown things. "Put her through her paces"? What ever did that mean? And who was Jim Karner? He must be very important if there was any doubt that that wonderful horse might not be good enough for him.

All Daisy's previous thoughts of going home and putting on the kettle for tea disappeared. There was only one place for her now – the paddock. Down the street she trotted, her own feet twinkling as she passed her own cottage, passed the baker's shop and turned left towards the paddock.

Jack, who was walking his horse round some smallish jumps, heard her and turned around. "Climb up on the gate," he called. "You'll see better."

Daisy, turning to put down her shopping, found herself confronting a large brown form.

It was Milly the cow who had waddled up, followed by a bevy of ducks. Her large tongue licked round her lips, her eyes bulging with spiteful curiosity.

"'Ee just wants you to look as stoopid as 'ee does stuck up on that horse."

"There are some, I know," said Daisy coldly, "who look even more stupid on the ground."

The ducks started to cackle with amusement, but Milly swished them into silence with her tail.

"Oh yes?" she said vulgarly. "Wellit's unnacherel, that's wot it is, so you needn't try to be clever with me, Daisy Pig."

But Daisy ignored her and climbing up the fence,

balanced herself precariously on the top rail.

Having walked the horse round all the jumps, Jack had now mounted, and quite magically, or so it seemed, the enchanted animal glided from a walk, to a trot and into a canter. Daisy almost fell off the gate in her admiration. He then set the horse at the first fence and, like a bird, she sailed over.

On she sped, dancing and prancing, until she and Jack had cleared every jump in the paddock.

"Oh, well *done!*" cried Daisy, and clapped ecstatically.

"Wot are *you* clapping at?" demanded Milly with her usual rudeness, shoving her head so roughly through the gate in order to see, that once again Daisy all but fell off.

"Can't see nothin' for you sittin' up there. Like a

bloomin' monkey up a stick," she added maliciously.

The ducks almost fell over themselves with mocking laughter. Daisy Pig like a monkey up a stick! What ever would she say? They decided to stay around and watch the sparks fly, but to their disappointment, Daisy said nothing. Instead she was watching Jack who had dismounted and was leading the beautiful horse over to the gate. The ducks saw him, too, and fled. Milly tried to pull her head back through the bars but it got stuck. Her eyes rolled round fearfully and her huge tongue protruded, licking around desperately.

"Not very bright, are you, old lady!" said Jack kindly, and handing the reins over to Daisy to hold, took Milly's large head in both hands, twisted it slightly to one side, and gently pushed it back through the bars. Safe on the other side, Milly glared at him angrily. Not very bright! Old Lady! Seeing her hesitate, Jack leaned over the gate and gave her a sharp tap on the rump.

"Off!" he said firmly. Milly knew better than to argue. She stalked off, bellowing loudly her indignation. Half-way, she turned round to glare in his direction, and then wished she had not, for there, sitting upon that elegant horse, was – Daisy Pig! Lumbering into a rocking canter, Milly stormed off into the blue.

Meanwhile Jack was leading his horse back to the stable.

Sally met them, her eyes shining. "What do you think of her, Daisy?" she called excitedly. "She's going to be perfect for the Gymkhana on Saturday. You are coming, aren't you? What a pity you can't get a horse, Daisy. You could have entered the jumping class for beginners!"

Sally disappeared into the dark of the stable. Jack went to fetch some hay and Daisy slowly made her way back to the cottage.

Several voices came in greeting but she walked on in a trance-like state. She sat down at the table and ate – well, what she ate she never could recall, for half-way through the meal an idea so brilliant and so simple, struck her that she shot up in self-admiration.

It consisted of only one word.

Victor.

With a scattering of crumbs and a hasty dab to her mouth, Daisy shot out of her cottage and almost ran towards the field where Vic's humble little house was.

To her delight he was out in the field, a woolly hat with bobbles on his head to protect it from the sun, whilst gently he rubbed his neck up and down against the wooden fence post.

"Victor!"

Dreamily Vic looked up. Coming towards him, waving gaily, was his friend Daisy Pig.

"Victor," she called again, in a tone of such sweetness that it made him feel slightly uncomfortable. He ambled slowly towards her and rested his head on the fence.

"Hello, Daisy," he said sleepily. But to his surprise, Daisy paid his greeting no heed. Instead she squeezed through the fence, then stepped well back.

"Now I want you to keep quite still, Victor," she commanded and began to eye him all over.

"You ain't going to be a nurse again, Daisy Pig?" he asked, looking over his shoulder nervously. "Like last time?"

But Daisy ignored his twittering.

"How are your legs?" she asked him at last, in tones of great gravity.

Vic, who had never thought of his legs separately from the rest of his body, looked at them in surprise.

"Wot's wrong with my legs?" he asked with a puzzled frown. "They're all there, aren't they?

Oi ain't lost one, 'ave oi?"

He thought this rather funny but Daisy frowned and held up a regal hand to silence him. The time had come, she felt, to divulge her plans. Well, part of them anyway.

"Victor," she said. "I have decided I *must* learn to ride."

Relief spread like sunshine over Vic's homely face.

"Oh, is that all? You had me really worried, you did, Daisy Pig. Oi thought you –," he hesitated to communicate the alarming picture that had crossed his mind of Daisy Pig bearing down on him in her nurse's uniform.

"Yes?" demanded Daisy, rather coldly. "You thought what?"

Vic shuffled uneasily wondering how he could get out of this tight corner. But then a second dreadful picture slid into his mind. "Ride?" he gulped. "Did oi hear you say 'ride'?"

"You did, indeed," smiled Daisy toothily. "So you see, I need a horse."

Vic felt the trembles coming on him.

"And guess," prattled on Daisy, coyly, "who I thought of first?"

Vic knew only too well, but he was desperate.

"Oi ain't given anyone rides since young Sally was a tot and she fell off, and screamed and screamed something awful. Me poor old 'ead ached all that day." He shuddered at the memory.

But Daisy was not interested in his memories or his headache.

"Well, that's all right, then," she announced cheerfully, "because *I* shan't fall off. So – can we start tomorrow? At nine?"

"Nine?" moaned Vic, as if he had just been given the time of his execution.

"And then you *must* have lunch with me," said Daisy.

Suddenly Vic saw a silver lining. His spirits, which had fallen to below floor level, began to rise. A light came back into his eyes.

"With lots of carrots, Daisy? And some of those nice apples from your tree? P'raps with real custard?"

Solemnly, Daisy Pig nodded three times.

A bargain had been struck and both knew it.

At nine sharp, Daisy, looking very fetching, or so she thought, in her white open-necked shirt, blue jeans and a hat borrowed from Sally, was down by Vic's field. Already, Vic was standing obligingly close to the fence.

"Good morning, Victor," trilled Daisy graciously. "And how are you?"

Without waiting for his reply, she clambered up the rails of the fence. Stretching out, she grabbed a handful of Vic's mane, and by sliding a leg out, found herself sitting on his broad back, almost up to the sky it seemed, for the ground beneath her could not be seen. It was one of the most exhilarating moments of her life, thought Daisy, happily. She fastened two hands firmly in Vic's mane and waited patiently. Nothing happened. She waited a little longer. Still nothing happened. She waited a little longer. At last, she could restrain herself no longer.

"Victor," she asked tetchily. "Shouldn't you be doing something? Like moving?"

Vic considered the matter. "No-o," he eventually responded. "T'ain't me. It's *you* wot should be doing something, Daisy Pig. *You're* supposed to be telling me wot to do – with your legs. But," he added kindly, "oi suppose, with little legs like yours, you can't do very much. Wot about you just telling me what to do and oi'll do it?"

"Oh!" Daisy, who had not been too pleased at being reminded so frankly of her "little" legs, was slightly mollified by the generosity of Vic's offer. "That *is* a good idea. I tell you what to do? I like that."

"Oi thought you might," said Vic, a little gloomily.

"Well then," enthused Daisy, "what about starting off with a walk?" and pitching her voice an octave higher than normal, she gave him the command "Walk!"

Unfortunately, just at that moment, one of the bobbles on Vic's hat had lodged in his ear, and he had to give his head a sharp shake to dislodge it.

Daisy leaned forward and repeated her command a little more sharply this time. Vic gave a start.

"Oo, sorry," he babbled. "Didn't really hear you the first time. Right. Oi'm walking now."

He stepped out so suddenly and so smartly that Daisy lost her balance. She gave a little scream and grabbed hold of even more of Vic's mane.

"Stop!" she cried. "Stop! Stop!" Vic stopped, whilst Daisy wriggled back to safety. "Do you have to wobble so much?" she complained bitterly. "How d'you expect anyone to stay on your back if it keeps slithering all over the place?"

Vic, knowing Daisy could not see, allowed himself a little grin.

"Sorry," he said. "Oi'll go more easily this time," but he gave a little titter.

"Very well," agreed Daisy, not very graciously, "but only when I tell you," and sitting up in a most dignified manner, she trilled out one more "Wa-alk."

This time Vic moved off. Plod, plod, plod, he went; round and round and round the field he went. In the heat of the day, his head sank lower and lower. Gradually the shuffling on his back ceased. Daisy was finding her seat. Her confidence began to soar.

"Isn't this wonderful?" she cried in elation. "Why, *why*, have I not done this before? Victor – I *really* think I'm ready to trot now!"

Vic, who was half asleep, came to with a snort. "Wot's that? Trot? Did you say 'trot', Daisy Pig?" he called out in sleepy confusion.

"I did," sang out Daisy, "so trot on, Victor! Trot."

Victor shambled into a trot.

Instantly Daisy's high spirits collapsed.

"Oo-oo-ooh!" she gasped, as she found herself bopping uncontrollably up and down on Vic's back. With each bop, little squeals of anguish burst from her lips. "Ouch!" she howled. "Ooh! Ow! Ooch!" and with each cry, Vic's grin grew broader.

Suddenly the bopping stopped. There came a long banshee-like wail, and something shot between his ears, dragging his hat over his eyes, leaving him in darkness, and then slid, squawking and clutching

down his nose only to land in a messy heap at his feet.
It was Daisy. For her, too, everything had gone
temporarily black.

"Where am I?" she cried out in a daze.

"Are you all right, Daisy?" asked Vic fearfully.
Daisy managed to shove her hat back onto her head.
Slowly, she struggled to her feet. As the pain
evaporated and her breath returned, she turned to
Vic, determined to give him a sharp piece of her
mind. But as her mouth opened, she spotted a large
brown head angling its way between the fence rails
and the large tongue came out of the lips as it
continued chewing.

It was Milly the cow. Daisy drew herself up with
dignity.

"I'm fine," she said brightly. "If I could get up

again, Victor, please."

A relieved Vic trotted up to the fence, while Daisy limped behind and then mounted once more. Holding his mane very tightly, she called out loudly and clearly enough for Milly to hear, "Walk, Victor."

Obediently, Vic walked and Daisy stayed put. With a cry of outrage, Milly the cow stumped back home to relate the horror of it all to the ducks.

After a hearty lunch, Vic lolled back in an easy chair, glowing with good food and good humour. He looked at Daisy sitting opposite to him, and said with affectionate pride, "Fancy your getting back on like that, Daisy old girl. How you did it oi'll never understand." His head wagged as he considered the mystery. "When young Sally fell off that time," he reminisced, "oi thought she'd never stop howlin'. But you – you just got up and climbed back on." His eyes shone with admiration.

It suddenly occurred to Daisy that Vic had obviously not seen Milly the cow. She smiled modestly and thanked him for his kind words. He beamed with such obvious pleasure that Daisy thought it might possibly be just the right moment to mention to him phase two of her plan.

"Dear Victor," she said sweetly, filling up his cup again, "if it hadn't been for you, I could not have done it. Yet as soon as I did, I knew, I just *knew* we would make a splendid team. A winning partnership."

She slipped a chocolate biscuit onto his empty plate.

Vic looked down. "Are you sure, Daisy Pig?" he asked, knowing that already he had eaten almost half of the biscuits.

Daisy beamed. "Of *course* I'm sure. You and I, Victor. Next Saturday – in the Beginners Jumping Class." She picked up the packet of biscuits. "Have the lot," she said generously.

"That's very kind of you," cried Victor, who adored chocolate biscuits. "Thank you."

"No," said Daisy, standing up. "It is I who should thank you. Oh, Victor, I'll – er, I mean *you*, you'll be wonderful! We'll practise all week. And on Saturday I'll show old –" she stopped. She had been about to say old Milly the cow, but thought better of it. "On Saturday," she began again, "*WE* shall show them all just how good we are!"

A feeling of unease came over Vic. Something, he felt, was going wrong again. He looked up. Daisy Pig seemed to tower above him, a strange light burning in her eyes. Suddenly the biscuit in his mouth lost its flavour. His jaw dropped. He began to feel distinctly unwell.

The day of the Gymkhana arrived bright and sunny. Sally came round. She combed Vic's mane and tail, polished his hooves, and helped Daisy to saddle him up. Then both of them rode down to the paddock where they inspected the jumps.

"You'll be in the first event," Sally said. "Take Vic into that corner over there and don't come out until you hear your name over the loudspeaker. You'll be after that girl over there on the big chestnut horse. D'you see her?"

Daisy nodded. "When your name is called, ride out into the ring and, when the bell goes, start jumping. All right? I really must go now. Good luck, Daisy." And Sally cantered off before she could even thank her or wish her good luck, too.

Daisy took Vic over to where a small knot of riders and horses had gathered and looked around. Some looked decidedly nervous but others seemed surprisingly cool and confident – none more so than the sharp-faced girl mounted on the chestnut.

A voice suddenly boomed over the loudspeaker and the group grew silent.

"Good morning, Ladies and Gentlemen. Event Number One is about to start. This is our Beginners Jumping Class, and who knows but we may have here amongst our young competitors a future world-class show-jumper."

The girl on the large chestnut smirked as though she thought it might possibly be her.

The voice over the loudspeaker spoke again.

"Our first competitor is Master George Fudge on Fatso."

Master George, legs flailing, set out. By simply listening to the crashing of fences and the cries of the

90

spectators, Daisy was able to follow his fortunes. He came out red-faced and crestfallen with sixteen faults. One by one the entrants dwindled until only Daisy and the girl on the chestnut were left.

"May we have the next competitor, please," called the voice over the loudspeaker. "Miss Amelia Twitt-Smithers on Pipsqueak."

And Miss Amelia Twitt-Smithers, head high as if about to claim her position as star-rider of the future, cantered out.

Pipsqueak was jumping well for ripple after ripple of applause followed them round, jump by jump. And then a hush fell on the crowd. It was obviously the last jump, the most difficult of them all. Miss Amelia set her mount squarely at the jump and spurred him on. Up he galloped and then, astonishingly, jammed on his brakes. Over his head and over the jump went the immaculate Miss Amelia Twitt-Smithers. She got up, disbelief written all over her face, seized her horse roughly by the reins and mounted again. Again they charged at the jump. Again Pipsqueak refused. One last time the rider wheeled him round, once more she put him to the jump, this time thrashing him with her riding crop. The mood of the spectators changed to one of anger and Pipsqueak, taking matters into his own hands, swerved around the gate, and galloped out of the ring. Miss Amelia Twitt-Smithers was disqualified. As she rode past Vic she snarled, "Get out of my way, *cart-horse*!"

A snigger reached Daisy's ear from the fence. Glancing round she caught sight of Milly the cow and her raggle-taggle of ducks.

"Look at her!" called out Milly. "'Oo does she think she is? Stuck up there like a pint of best milk."

"Or like a monkey up a stick," giggled the ducks. "Just like a . . ." but the loudspeaker drowned them and their quacking out.

"Our last competitor, Miss Daisy Pig on Victor," boomed the voice. A hush fell over the crowd.

Daisy sat tall. She'd show Milly the cow, she vowed. Vic drew himself up. Cart-horse, indeed. Well, what if he was? He'd show 'em!

The bell went. Vic began to go backwards. "What are you doing?" hissed Daisy, panicking. "You're going the wrong way!"

"Oi'm just getting a run in," hissed Vic in reply.

Back, back he went. Milly the cow hastily pulled back her head as Vic's hindquarters came ever on. At the fence he stopped and then gathered himself for the great charge.

For one of the ducks, however, it was a chance too good to miss. He thrust his head out and gleefully took a sharp nip at Victor's unsuspecting back leg.

With a wild neigh, Vic leapt forward with Daisy just managing to hold on.

Over the first fence they flew, over the brush, over the triple, round and over the water jump. At each jump, Daisy and Vic parted company but by hanging on grimly to the reins, Daisy managed to find herself back in the saddle. On they went; three more jumps and now the last gate.

"Calm down, Vic!" someone called out from the crowd. It was Sally. Vic paused, took a deep breath, and then cantering on, jumped for his life. His hind foot caught the top rail. It rose. The crowd cried "Oh!" in horror. And then it fell, rocking gently, back into place. "Ah!" cried the crowd and suddenly everyone was clapping and cheering.

The loudspeaker crackled into life, and a voice said very calmly, "Miss Daisy Pig and Victor. Clear round – which makes them the winners."

Again the crowd went wild. The gentleman behind the speaker mopped his brow. "Most extraordinary riding I've ever seen. Must be some new-fangled style, but, by jove, it worked!"

And then he came down to present the prizes. To Vic a large red rosette with a golden "First" on. For Daisy a silver cup saying "Winner of the Beginners Jumping Event".

As they trotted away Daisy said knowingly to Vic, "Of course, *that* was Mr Jim Karner."

But Vic really was not listening. Today, he knew he would never do it again. But tomorrow – with someone like Daisy Pig?

"Home, Victor," said Daisy, happily. "Time for tea."